# STARTING SOCCER

## Helen Edom and Mike Osborne

(Mike Osborne is a Senior Lecturer in Physical Education and Sport at the West London Institute of Higher Education.)

### Edited by Harriet Castor

 ### Designed by Maria Wheatley and Carol Law

### Illustrated by Norman Young

## Contents

# About soccer

Soccer is one of the most popular and exciting ball games in the world. This book shows you the skills you need to play. You can find out how to tackle, shoot and head the ball. There are tips on goalkeeping and goal scoring, plus tricks to help you outwit your opponents.

Here you can see a match going on. The two teams are trying to kick or head the ball into each other's goal.

Players need to be able to run fast and turn quickly.

The referee wears black so that he stands out from the players.

The referee must be careful not to get in the way.

Players on opposite teams try to get the ball away from each other. This is called tackling.

White lines mark out the different areas of the soccer field.

One player in each team is the captain. He tells players what to do.

The outfit a player wears is called a uniform.

Goal

The goalkeepers change ends halfway through the game. This is after a break called half-time.

The goalkeeper wears a different shirt so that he can be seen easily.

**The whole team works together. Players should watch out for their team mates.**

## What you need to play

The first thing you need for soccer is a ball. You can buy one in any shop selling sports goods. They are made of plastic or leather. Plastic ones are lighter, so they are easier to start with.

For soccer practice, you can wear any comfortable clothes and non-slip shoes. To play a match you will need soccer cleats. There are different kinds for grass and other surfaces.

Cleats for playing on grass have studs on the bottom to stop you from slipping.

**Stud**

## Where to play

You can learn soccer skills in any safe, open space away from roads. Make sure that there is nothing to break nearby such as a window or greenhouse.

## World champions

Every four years countries play each other in the World Cup. The winners are world champions.

**The World Cup trophy**

3

# Using your feet

Unless you are a goalkeeper, you will use your feet most of the time to make the ball do what you want.

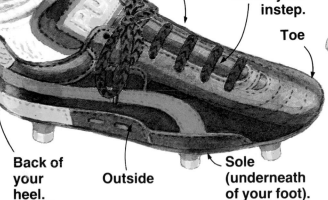

Inside

This area is called your instep.

Toe

Back of your heel.

Outside

Sole (underneath of your foot).

See how you can move the ball with different parts of your foot. Use your toe, heel, sole, the inside and the outside. Try this with each foot.

Using instep.

Using inside of foot.

You can make the ball go farther by kicking with your instep. But it's easier to make it go where you want if you use the inside of your foot.

## First kicks

Imagine a line cutting the ball in half from side to side. To make it go straight and low, kick the ball on this line.

Use the inside of your foot.

Kick the ball here.

If you kick below the line, the ball flies up in the air. This makes it harder to aim.

The ball was kicked here.

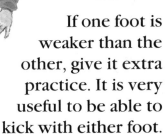

If one foot is weaker than the other, give it extra practice. It is very useful to be able to kick with either foot.

# Close control

You need to learn to control the ball really well to stop other players from taking it away from you. These activities will help.

Start by rolling the ball around with the sole of your foot, any way you like. Try this with each foot.

**Keep this leg relaxed.**

# Inside and outside

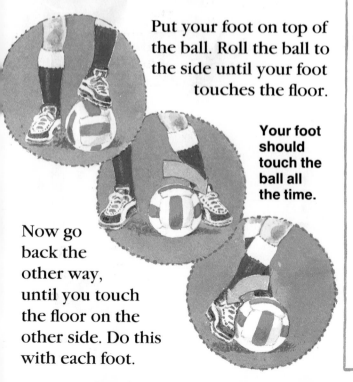

Put your foot on top of the ball. Roll the ball to the side until your foot touches the floor.

**Your foot should touch the ball all the time.**

Now go back the other way, until you touch the floor on the other side. Do this with each foot.

# Juggling

This is good ball control practice. First throw the ball into the air and let it bounce once.

**Throw the ball about this high.**

As it rises, gently kick it straight up in the air. See how many times you can kick it again before it falls on the ground.

**Use the top of your foot.**

Sometimes players use their chest or legs instead of their feet. See if you can keep the ball in the air with your thigh like this.

# Dribbling

Dribbling, or running with the ball, is a very important skill. It lets you get into a good position to kick to a team mate, or to score a goal.

First, stand still and tap the top of the ball with each foot in turn. See if you can do this without looking.

**— The ball stays still.**

Now try moving with the ball. Nudge it with the insides and outsides of your feet.

**Using the outside of the foot.**

**Using the inside of the foot.**

**Try not to stop moving as you kick the ball.**

Keep the ball slightly ahead of you. This means you can see it and keep a look out for other players.

## Pelé

Pelé was one of the most famous soccer players ever. He had spectacular dribbling skills. These helped him keep the ball long enough to score 1,283 goals.

**Pelé played for Brazil 111 times.**

Don't let the ball get too far ahead, though, or another player may reach it before you.

**This player has stolen the ball.**

## Dribbling races

Mark a spot with a coat. Try racing to it and back. See how fast you can go and keep control. Try not to slow down when you turn.

**Arms out for balance.**

**Legs loose, relaxed and slightly bent.**

**Look where you are going.**

**Don't stop running as you kick the ball.**

See if you can zig-zag the ball in and out of a line of coats or bags. Use the insides and outsides of your feet to make the ball go different ways.

## Watching out

This is a game for two. It helps you look out for other players while you are dribbling.

Dribble a ball each. Keep an eye out for the other player.

If one person puts up a hand the other has to stop. If you miss the signal the other player scores a mark.

**Both players can give signals.**

You can also point in any direction. The other player must turn that way. If he doesn't, you score a mark.

**Keep the ball under control so you can turn or stop quickly.**

# Passing the ball

Good soccer teams pass the ball from one player to another. This helps them get the ball nearer to their opponents' goal so that one of their players can score.

## Short pass

When you pass, aim the ball carefully. It needs to go to the right person, not someone from the other team.

**It's easier to aim with the inside of your foot.**

Put one foot alongside the ball. Turn your body a little to the side.

**This foot faces forward.**

**Leg keeps moving.**

Kick the middle of the ball with your other foot. Let your leg swing up as the ball moves.

## Cushioning the ball

When someone passes the ball to you, move your foot back as the ball hits it. This stops the ball from bouncing off. This is called cushioning the ball.

**Foot moves back.**

## Wedging the ball

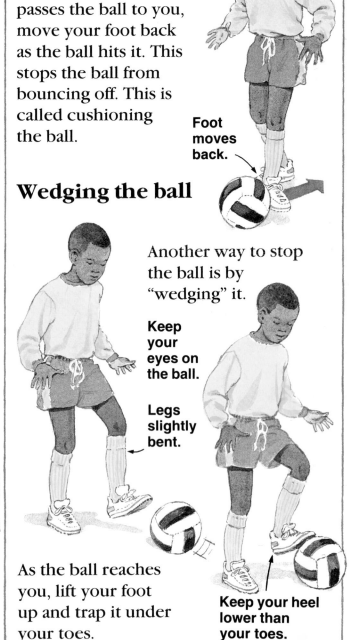

Another way to stop the ball is by "wedging" it.

**Keep your eyes on the ball.**

**Legs slightly bent.**

As the ball reaches you, lift your foot up and trap it under your toes.

**Keep your heel lower than your toes.**

# Improving your aim

Ask a friend to stand a little way away. Try passing the ball to each other. See if you can pass with just two touches: one to stop the ball and one to pass it back.

To make this harder, put a pair of coats between you. See if you can pass the ball between the coats.

## Aiming at the goal

**Low shots can be tricky to reach.**

If you are near the goal, you can score using the side of your foot. Aim the ball away from the goalkeeper.

# Passing game

One player has the ball. The rest jog around her in a big circle.

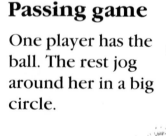

**Don't let the ball go out of the circle.**

**Keep the game going quite quickly.**

Someone in the circle raises a hand. The person with the ball passes to him.

He then dribbles into the middle and gets ready to pass to someone else.

9

# Farther and faster

You can kick the ball harder and farther if you use your instep (see page 4). This is useful for long passes or for scoring goals.

**Try to place your non-kicking foot alongside the ball.**

**Arms out for balance.**

**Instep**

Start behind and to one side of the ball. Then run up and kick it as hard as you can with your instep.

Kick with your toe down. Keep both knees slightly bent. Let your leg swing up after kicking.

## Scoring practice

**Passer**

Try this scoring practice with some friends. One person is the shooter and one is the passer. The others collect the balls.

**Try to shoot without stopping the ball first.**

**Shooter**

**It's best if you can use several balls.**

**Collectors roll the balls back to the passer.**

The shooter stands 15-20m (16-22yds) from the goal. The passer passes the ball just in front of the shooter.

The shooter runs forward and kicks the ball into the goal. Take turns at being the shooter and the passer.

## Stopping high balls

Powerful passes may bounce, or go high. You can use different parts of your body to stop the ball.

Push out your chest to meet the ball.

Use the top part of your chest.

**Using your thigh.**

**Using the top of your foot.**

Sag back to cushion the ball.

Remember to cushion the ball. Bring your foot or leg down as the ball touches, to stop it from bouncing away again.

You can use your chest too. Spread your arms and stick your chest out. Sag back and down as the ball touches.

## Two touch

In this soccer game players can only touch the ball twice in a row. This gives you a lot of passing practice.

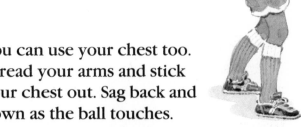

Think how you are going to pass each time.

You can aim short passes carefully with the side of your foot.

You could mark out goals with coats or bags.

Using the top of your foot is harder, but it's good for long shots.

11

# Using your head

If the ball is high in the air, you can use your forehead to send it where you want. This is called heading.

## Throw-head-catch game

Three players stand in a triangle. The first person throws the ball, the second heads it and the third catches it. Carry on like this around the triangle.

**Second person**

**First person**

**Turn to make the ball go in the right direction.**

**Third person**

## Warming up

Heading uses your neck muscles a lot so you must warm them up first.

Push your forehead against your hand. Try to stiffen your neck muscles.

Tilt your head and push it sideways against your hand. Do this to each side.

Drop your chin and roll your head slowly from side to side.

## Heading practice

Hold the ball up in both hands. Pull your elbows back and push your head forward.

Keep your eyes on the ball.

**Use a fairly soft ball at first.**

**Elbows out to the sides.**

Grit your teeth so you don't bite your tongue.

As your head touches the ball, let go of it. Stiffen your neck and push the ball with your forehead.

After some practice, ask a friend to toss you the ball gently. See if you can head it back.

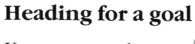

## A long header

This is a useful way to send the ball away from your goal. Jump up to it, arching your back.

**Keep your eyes on the ball.**

Push your head and body forward so you hit the ball in the middle of your forehead.

Hit the bottom half of the ball so it rises over the other players' heads.

## Heading for a goal

You may get a chance to score a goal with a header. Try to head the ball down into the goal. This may be harder for the goalkeeper to save.

## Heading match

You can play this with two teams of three or more players.

**Use coats or bags to mark out the goals.**

Head or throw the ball to each other instead of kicking. But you can only score goals by heading (not throwing).

13

# Getting the ball

Trying to take the ball away from another player is called tackling. You must get the ball without tripping the other player or using your hands.

## Jockeying

If an opponent has the ball, you can jockey him. Keep about 1m (1yd) in front of him. This slows him down and he may make mistakes.

**Be ready to tackle (see how on the right).**

## Tackling

It is easiest to tackle someone if you start to one side. This forces the person to change direction.

**Having to turn may put the player off balance.**

Try to kick the ball just before your opponent does. You may need to flick the ball over his foot.

**Bend your knees and crouch slightly over the ball.**

Make sure you know where you are going next. Be ready to dribble, shoot or pass to another player.

**Move away quickly.**

## Guarding

Help you team by guarding an opponent. Stay just behind her. If the ball is passed to her, go forward to tackle, or steal it before it reaches her.

14

# Piggy in the middle

**This player has just stolen the ball.**

Two players pass the ball back and forth to each other. A third stands in between and tries to get the ball.

If she does, one of the others takes a turn in the middle. Watch for a chance to steal the ball this way in a match.

## Sliding tackle

Sometimes soccer stars kick the ball away with a sliding tackle. Players need to be very fit to do this without injuring themselves.

# Tackling game

Test your skills with two or more friends. Mark out four corners of a square with coats or stones.

**Watch out in case someone sneaks your ball away as you tackle another player.**

**If you are out, keep busy with some juggling practice (see page 3).**

Each dribble a ball inside the square. At the same time, try to kick someone else's ball out of the square.

If your ball goes outside the square, you must drop out of the game. The winner is the last player left.

# Beating your guard

If you have the ball, players on the other team will try to take it away from you.

Here are some ways to get past them without losing the ball.

## Sneaky moves

**You actually go this way.**

**It looks like you are going this way.**

A good trick is to pretend to go one way, but then go another. First lean as if you are going to move one way.

Your guard will move to block you. As soon as he does, shift your weight the other way and run off past him.

Your guard is off-balance. This gives you time to get away. It is called "wrong-footing" your guard.

## Pretend pass

Another trick is to pretend you are going to pass to a team mate.

**Team mate.**

**The pass would go this way.**

**Guard**

Your guard will move to block the pass.

Now you can run quickly past your guard.

## Cruyff turn

Johan Cruyff used this trick when he played for Holland in the 1974 World Cup finals.

Pretend you are about to kick the ball forward.

Instead, lift your foot over the ball and flick it behind you.

**Don't let the ball go too far.**

Now quickly turn and take the ball the other way.

**Your opponent is left standing.**

## Crab alley game

Mark out an alley with pairs of coats like this. There is a crab (defender) by each pair.

Crabs are tummy-up, on hands and feet. They can only move sideways between their two coats.

**Leave a gap of 8–10m (9–11yds) between the coats.**

Try and dribble around each crab. Use the tricks on this page to help you.

The crabs try to kick the ball away from you. They must not use their hands.

17

# Goalkeeping

Goalkeeping is a very important job. You have to concentrate and act quickly. You can either catch the ball or knock it away. It's best to catch it if you can. Then your opponents cannot kick it again.

## Catching safely

**Keep thumbs close together to catch a high ball.**

**Keep little fingers close together to pick up a low ball.**

When you catch the ball spread your fingers out like this. Keep your hands close together so the ball cannot slip through.

Pull the ball in to your chest as you catch it. This helps stop it from bouncing away.

**This is a goal.**

When you save the ball, you must keep hold of it. If you drop it behind the goal line it counts as a goal.

## Catching circle

This game gives you catching practice. One player throws the ball and then calls a name. That person has to be quick to catch the ball.

The catcher then throws and calls another name. This game gets harder if you use two or more balls at once.

## Holding on

See how good you are at holding the ball. Try picking it up and then doing a forward roll still holding it.

## Body barrier

**Your chest stops the ball.**

**Legs stop the ball if it slips through your hands.**

**Keep your knee and heel close together so the ball will not roll through.**

You can use your body as an extra barrier. If you miss with your hands, you will still stop the ball.

If the ball is rolling slowly you can bend down and pick it up, keeping your feet together.

If the ball is rolling faster, turn your feet sideways and bend down on one knee to catch it.

## High and low

**Jumping for the ball.**

**Keep your eyes on the ball all the time.**

**Diving for the ball.**

Sometimes you need to jump up to catch a high ball. You will go higher if you take off from one foot.

You may have to dive for the ball, too. Try diving from your knees first. Then try from a crouching position.

## Wearing gloves

Goal shots are often hard and powerful. Gloves help stop the ball from stinging your hands.

# More about goalkeeping

Once you have saved the ball you need to make sure the other team cannot get it again. Throw, roll or kick it to a team mate. Do this quickly before your opponents guess where you are going to send the ball.

## Rolling the ball

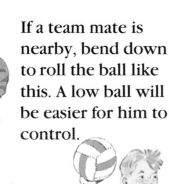

If a team mate is nearby, bend down to roll the ball like this. A low ball will be easier for him to control.

## Throwing

The ball will go more quickly if you throw it. For a short throw, bend your elbow and push the ball forward.

You can throw the ball farther like this. Take your arm right back and keep it straight as you throw.

## Kicking

To kick the ball a long way, drop it gently from waist-height and kick it with your instep.

**Instep**

Another way is to drop the ball and let it bounce once before you kick it.

**Kick the ball just as it begins to rise.**

## Choosing the right player

Don't send the ball to a guarded player. The guard may manage to take the ball away from him.

**This player is a good choice.**

**This player is guarded.**

## Pushing the ball away

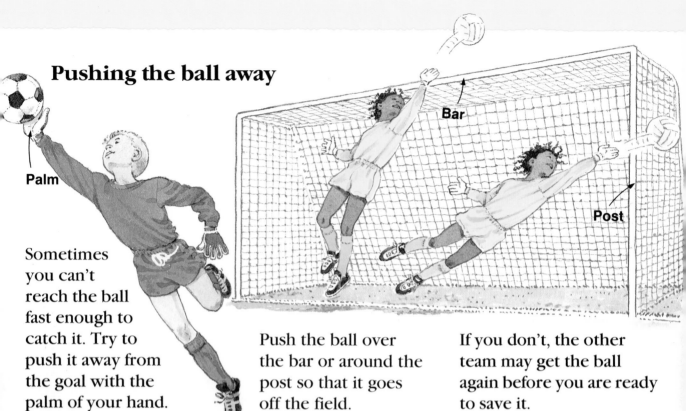

**Palm**

**Bar**

**Post**

Sometimes you can't reach the ball fast enough to catch it. Try to push it away from the goal with the palm of your hand.

Push the ball over the bar or around the post so that it goes off the field.

If you don't, the other team may get the ball again before you are ready to save it.

## Coming out

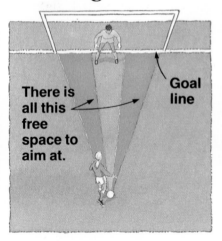

There is all this free space to aim at.

Goal line

The free space is narrower.

Don't stay too near the goal line. This leaves more room for players to shoot the ball past you.

If you come out a little you can reach the ball more easily, wherever the attacker shoots it.

Be careful not to come out too soon or too far. The attacker may get the ball around or over you.

# Playing as a team

Soccer is a team game. It is just as important to help a team mate get or keep the ball as to get the ball yourself.

If a team mate is closely guarded, it may be risky for her to keep the ball. Make it easy for her to pass to you. Try not to get in line, or level with her. Her guard may then block the pass.

**Guard**

Help the person with the ball by calling so she knows where other players are.

**This player is not in line. He is easier to pass to.**

**This player is in line. The guard is in the way.**

If a guard is coming up behind, shout "Man on!" as a warning.

## Wall pass

**Guard**

**Guard**

Here's how two players can outwit an opponent. If a guard tries to get the ball, one player passes it to the other.

The guard turns toward the player with the ball. The first player then runs around the guard into a clear space.

Now her team mate can pass back to her. This is called a wall pass because the ball goes to and fro as if it is bouncing off a wall.

22

# Cross-over play

**Face your team mate.**

**Your team mate keeps her body between the ball and the guard.**

**Kick with the side of the foot.**

You can use this trick to help a team mate who is being guarded very closely. Both of you run toward each other.

As you pass each other, your team mate kicks the ball into your path. Now you can get the ball safely away.

## Attackers and defenders

Before the game, players decide where they will play on the field.

**Defenders**

The sides of the field are called the wings.

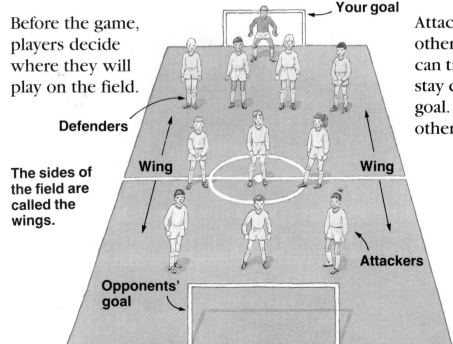

**Your goal**

**Wing**

**Wing**

**Attackers**

**Opponents' goal**

Attackers stay close to the other team's goal, so that they can try to score. Defenders stay close to their own goal. They try to stop the other team from scoring.

Some players stay in the middle, ready to help both attackers and defenders. They use the wings to get around the other team.

23

# Playing fairly

Rules help make soccer safe and enjoyable. If you break a rule the referee will give the ball to the other team to kick. This is called a free kick.

## Fouls

Breaking a rule is called a foul. Kicking, pushing or tripping a player or touching the ball with your hands (unless you are the goalkeeper) are all fouls.

**If the tackler kicks the player's leg and not the ball, this is a foul.**

## Direct and indirect free kicks

There are two sorts of free kick. The referee gives them for different types of foul. Free kicks are taken as close as possible to where the foul happened.

With direct free kicks, the kicker can shoot at the goal. These are given for serious fouls.

**A line like this is called a wall.**

Indirect free kicks are for less serious fouls. The kicker cannot score right away. He must pass the ball to another player first.

**Opponents can try to stop the ball but they must stand at least 9m (10yds) away from it.**

**This player is taking a direct free kick.**

24

# Being offside

This is a tricky rule to understand. It only applies at the moment when the ball is kicked to you.

The rule says you must not be the closest person to the goal you are aiming for. Two or more of the other team must be either level with you, or closer to the goal.

The goalkeeper counts as one opponent.

If the ball is kicked to her, this player is not offside.

If the ball is kicked to her, this player is offside.

If they are not, you are offside. The referee will give an indirect free kick to the other team.

## Ejection

If a player keeps breaking the rules the referee warns him. If he takes no notice the referee may eject him from the field.

In professional games, the referee shows a yellow card for a warning and a red card for an ejection.

## Penalty kick

Around the goal is the penalty area. If a serious foul happens there, the referee gives a penalty kick. It is taken from a place called the penalty spot.

Only the goalkeeper can try to stop the ball.

Penalty spot

# Playing eleven-a-side

In most professional matches, there are eleven players on each team. A match lasts for 90 minutes, with a ten minute break at half-time.

## Kick-off

There is a kick-off at the start of a match, after half-time, and every time a goal is scored.

**Halfway line**

**The ball is placed on this spot.**

At the start of a match a coin is tossed to decide which team kicks the ball first. After a goal, the team that didn't score takes the kick-off.

The referee puts the ball on a spot exactly in the middle of the field. Then the referee blows the whistle and one player kicks the ball.

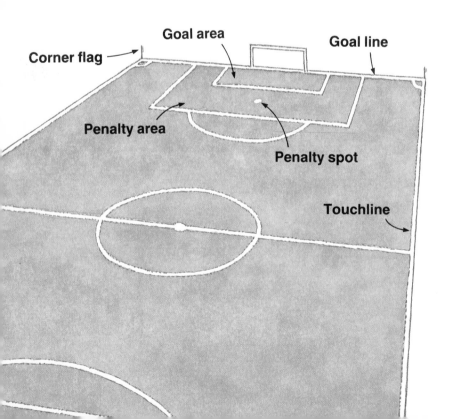

**Corner flag**

**Goal area**

**Goal line**

**Penalty area**

**Penalty spot**

**Touchline**

## Going off the field

Lines mark the sides of the field. On the long sides they are called touchlines. On the short sides they are called goal lines.

If you knock the ball over one of them, the referee stops the game and gives the ball to the other team. How the game starts again depends on which line the ball crossed.

**You must use both hands for a throw-in.**

**Stand outside the touchline.**

# Throw-in

If the ball crossed a touchline, it is thrown back onto the field. This is called a throw-in. You stand where the ball crossed the line, and throw from behind your head.

# Corner kick

If you knock the ball over your own goal line, the other team has a direct free kick (see page 24). It is taken from the corner circle.

**The shooter aims for the goal.**

**Corner circle**

# Goal kick

If you knock the ball over the other team's goal line (but it isn't a goal), they take a goal kick. This is a kick from a corner of the goal area.

**Goal area**

# Linesman

There is a linesman outside each touchline. He helps decide exactly where the ball crossed the line. He also helps decide if a player is offside (see page 25).

# Managers and coaches

A team's manager and coach watch from the bench. The manager runs the team and picks players for matches. The coach trains them.

# Smaller teams

Soccer is often just as much fun to play with small teams. You can have a good game with any number of players from three to seven-a-side. These are called small-sided games. They are very much like eleven-a-side games but with some important differences.

Small-sided games are played on a smaller field than eleven-a-side soccer. This means they can often be played indoors.

**There are semi-circles instead of boxes in front of each goal.**

**The goals are smaller than usual.**

**Two of these fields can fit side-by-side onto an eleven-a-side field.**

## Time

Small-sided games are usually quite short. Each half may only last for six or seven minutes. But if the score is equal at the end, the game may go on until another goal is scored.

Instead of a kick-off (see page 26), the referee drops the ball between two players, one from each team.

The referee restarts the game like this if the ball goes over the touchline. This is instead of a throw-in (see page 27).

## Keeping the ball low

The ball must not go above head height. If you kick it too high, the other team gets an indirect free kick (see page 24).

**Keeping the ball low helps stop windows from being broken inside.**

28

## Goal area

The semi-circle in front of each goal is the goal area. Only the goalkeeper is allowed in this area.

When goalkeepers are outside their goal area, they are only allowed to kick the ball. They cannot touch it with their hands.

## Penalty shoot-out

If there is a draw, there may be a penalty shoot-out. The teams take the same number of penalty kicks (see page 25). The team that scores the most goals wins.

**Only the goalkeeper can defend.**

## Scoring goals

There is no offside rule (see page 25) to worry about in small-sided soccer. But you can only shoot at goal from outside the goal area.

**Goal area**

## Indoor cleats

Indoor games are played on a smooth surface. You need cleats with crinkly soles to give you a good grip.

**Indoor soccer cleats.**

# Keeping fit and healthy

Soccer is fun, but it can be hard work too. Always warm up your muscles before you play. If you don't, you might strain or injure them. This could stop you from playing for weeks.

## Muscles

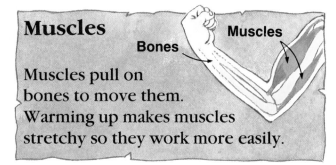

**Bones** **Muscles**

Muscles pull on bones to move them. Warming up makes muscles stretchy so they work more easily.

## Warming up

Start warming up by walking briskly to the field. Next, try some gentle jogging.

**Jogging backward.**

**Swing your arms.**

You could turn and jog backward, too. After a few minutes, try some exercises.

## Ankle circles

Lift one foot off the floor. Draw a circle in the air with your toe, first one way and then the other. Do this with each foot.

## Calf stretch

Put one foot behind you, keeping your leg straight. Bend the other leg until you feel a stretch. Count to eight then change legs.

**You should feel a stretch here.**

**Both feet point forward.**

**Both heels stay on the ground.**

## Groin stretch

Stand with your feet very wide apart, and bend one knee. Hold, then change legs. This stretches the muscles right at the top of your legs.

**Heels stay down.**

**Always stretch gently.**

## Back of thigh

Put one leg out straight in front and bend the other knee. Lean forward until you feel a stretch. Count to eight and then change legs.

**Keep your back very straight.**

**Push your bottom out behind you.**

**Feel a stretch in the back of your thigh.**

## Front of thigh

Stand on one leg. Bend the other up behind you.

**Hold this arm out to help you balance.**

**Keep this knee slightly bent.**

Grip the ankle and gently pull your foot up. Hold, then change legs.

## Side stretch

Reach up with one hand as high as you can. You will feel a stretch down your side.

**Looking up helps this stretch.**

Count to eight and then stretch your other side.

## Shoulders

Lift your shoulders up to your ears. Then let them drop back down. Do this a few times.

## After play

Your muscles are very hot after playing. Put on a sweater so they don't cool down too quickly. If you can, have a warm bath or shower.

# Index

## Useful addresses

**The Football Association,**
16 Lancaster Gate,
London, W2 3LW,
England.

**United States Soccer
Federation,**
1801–1811 S. Prairie
Avenue, Chicago,
IL 60616, USA.

**Australian Soccer
Federation,**
1st floor,
23-25 Frederick Street,
Rockdale, NSW 2216,
Australia.

**Canadian Soccer
Association,**
1600 James Naismith
Drive, Gloucester,
Ontario, K1B 5N4,
Canada.

**New Zealand Football
Association,**
P.O. Box 62–532,
Central Park, Auckland 6,
New Zealand.

Usborne Publishing would like to thank the children from Radstock Primary School who demonstrated the positions in this book.

First published in 1993 by Usborne House, 83-85 Saffron Hill, London, EC1N 8RT. England. Copyright © 1993 Usborne Publishing Ltd. First published in America March 1994.

Printed in Belgium.